For my niece Elzė. All of this hard work was done for you.
E.S.

First published in Great Britain and in the USA in 2016 by Frances Lincoln Children's Books,
74-77 White Lion Street, London N1 9PF, UK
QuartoKnows.com
Visit our blogs at QuartoKnows.com

A catalogue record for this book is available from the British Library.

ISBN 978-1-84780-879-0

Illustrated in gouache and digitally

Published by Rachel Williams • Edited by Katy Flint and Harriet Balfour-Evans
Designed by Andrew Watson • Production by Kate Pimm

Printed in China

1 3 5 7 9 8 6 4 2

giving thanks

more than **100** ways to say **thank you**

illustrated by
ellen surrey

Frances Lincoln
Children's Books

Hi! I'm Andy. When I was asked if there was anyone I would like to thank, these are the people I thought of.

Who would you like to say thank you to?

My mom

My dad

My brother

My sister

My grandpa

My grandma

What would you like to say thank you for?

Loving me

Making my dinner

Keeping me company

Playing games with me

Reading me a bedtime story

Encouraging me to do my best

Teaching me new things

ABC?

If you could give them a gift, what would you give?

An apron

A magic wand

A guidebook

ITALY

A pencil case

A stethoscope

A ball

A flashlight

A snorkel

Some chocolates

A magnifying glass

A ball

A telescope

A new book

A pack of cards

Another teddy

If you could do anything for them, what would you do?

Make them breakfast

Draw them a picture

Share your favorite thing with them

Make them laugh

Write them a thank-you card

COACH

Give them a treat

Help them out

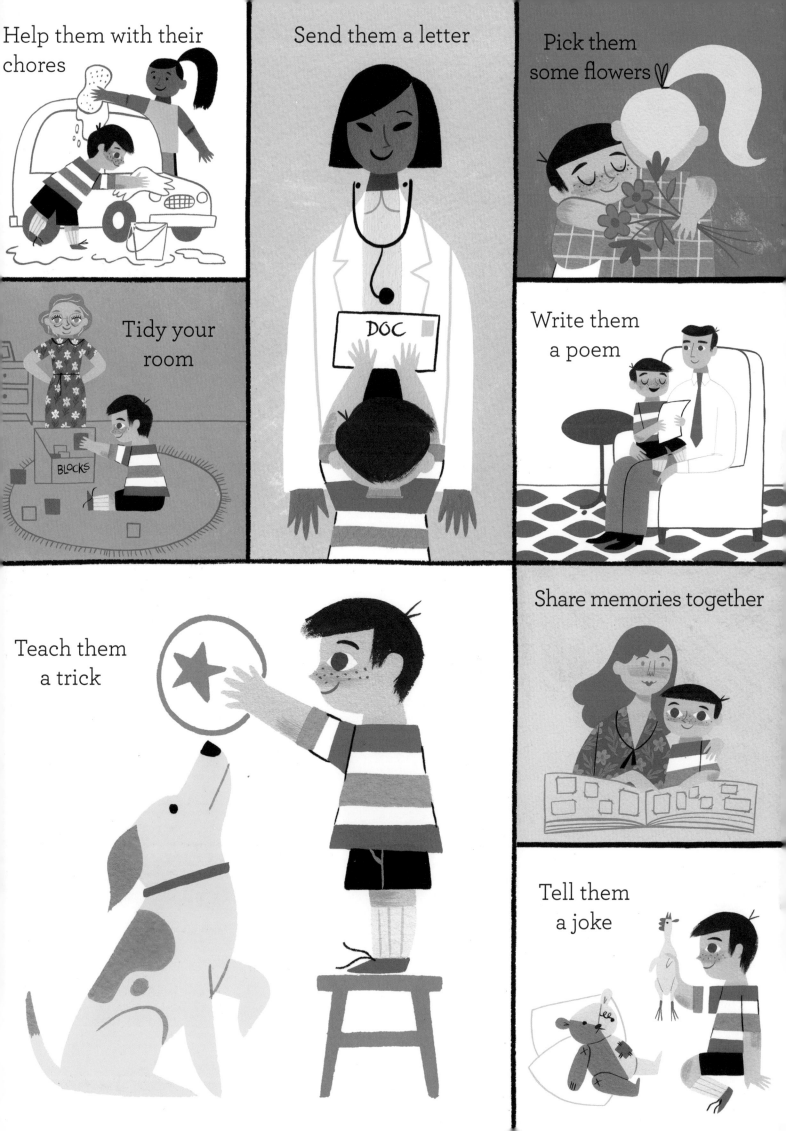

Help them with their chores

Send them a letter

Pick them some flowers

Tidy your room

DOC

Write them a poem

Teach them a trick

BLOCKS

Share memories together

Tell them a joke

If you could give them something to wear, what would it be?

A scarf

A new collar

A space suit

A dress

A pair of gloves

A bow tie

A rain jacket

An outfit for playing dress-up

A pair of shoes

A coat

A backpack

A pair of binoculars

A pair of sports socks

A magician's hat

A wet suit

If you could give them a vehicle, what would it be?

A scooter

A go-cart

A Jeep

A flying car

A hot air balloon

A limousine

A sled

A bicycle

A horse

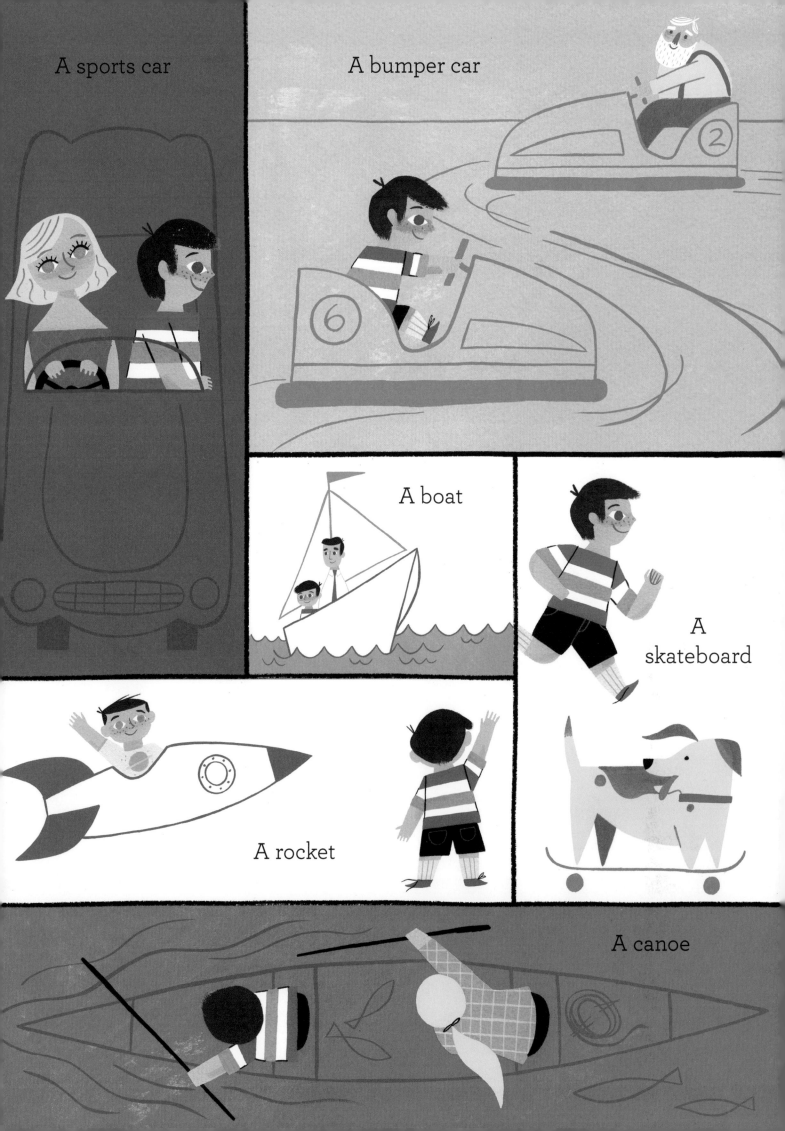

A sports car

A bumper car

A boat

A skateboard

A rocket

A canoe

If you could take them anywhere, where would you go?

The moon!

The woods

The South Pole

A five-star hotel

Up a mountain

A castle

The World Cup

Hollywood

A lighthouse

The carnival

The lake

A magic show

The beach

The rain forest

On a safari

Toasted marshmallows

Popcorn

A banana

Magic beans

High tea

Cotton candy

A bone

French fries

If you could give them a feeling, what would you give them?

Relaxed

Lucky

Excited

Loved

Out of this world

Sunny

Special

Proud

Happy

Magical

Cheerful

Brave

Terrific

Pleased

Inspired

Now it's your turn!
Make your own gratitude jar.

Write some colorful thank-you notes for all the good things in your life. See if you can fill your jar with thankfulness!

You will need:
- 1 jar (clean)
- colorful pens or pencils
- paper

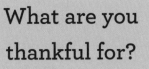

What are you thankful for?

Your pets

If you don't have a pet at home, name a friend's pet who you like playing with.

The food you eat

What is your favorite food? Name the person who cooks you the best dinners.

The weather

Do you like sunny days?
Or splashing in
puddles when
it rains?

Nature

Do you have a garden?
Or a park you like to
play in? Name some
plants or animals you
like that live there.

Your friends

Do you have a friend
who cheers you up
when you are sad?
What was the last game
you played together?

Your school

Who is your
favorite teacher?
Write down the
last new thing
you learned.

Your achievements

Write down a time when
you tried really hard. What
have you done, or made,
that you're proud of?

The people who help you

Name some people who
make you feel better.

Your family

Who gives the best hugs?
List some other things
your family does for you.

Your hobbies

Do you like playing sports?
How about music?
Does someone nice teach
you how to do these things?

Make thank-you cards for all your friends and family!

Create and write thank-you cards for the important people in your life. How many people can you make feel special?

You will need:
- paper
- scissors
- glue or tape
- pens and pencils

Who are you thankful for?

For your dad

Find and stick a favorite picture of you both on the front cover.

For your babysitter

Cut out a heart shape and stick it on the front. Collage the middle with scraps of paper.

For your sister

Press a flower and stick it to the front with tape.

For your mom

Write an IOU to do something nice for her.

For your teacher

Find an interesting leaf, cover it with paint, and use it to print leafy pictures.

For your teddy bear

Write them an invitation to a teddy bear's picnic.

For your best friend

Make them a ticket to a fun event.

For your grandma or grandpa

Cover your hand in paint and glitter to make a handprint.

For your doctor

Draw them dressed as a superhero!

For your cousin

Write them a funny joke and illustrate it with cartoons.